DATE DUE

D1068625

First published in Spain by Editorial Flamboyant S.L in 2017 under the title El gran libro de los superpoderes

English language edition published in 2020 by Beaming Books, an imprint of 1517 Media.

25 24 23 22 21 20   1 2 3 4 5 6 7 8

ISBN: 978-1-5064-6319-3

Library of Congress Cataloging-in-Publication Data

Names: Isern, Susanna, author. | Bonilla, Rocio, 1970- illustrator.
Title: The big book of superpowers / by Susanna Isern ; illustrated by
   Rocio Bonilla.
Other titles: Gran libro de los superpoderes. English
Description: English language edition. | Minneapolis : Beaming Books, 2020.
   | Originally published in Spanish: Barcelona : Flamboyant, 2017 under
   the title, El gran libro de los superpoderes. | Audience: Ages 5-8. |
   Summary: "With eighteen stories of kids with everyday superpowers, The
   Big Book of Superpowers will inspire kids to look inside and find what
   makes them extraordinary!"-- Provided by publisher.
Identifiers: LCCN 2019048110 | ISBN 9781506463193 (hardcover)
Subjects: LCSH: Ability in children--Juvenile literature. |
   Individuality--Juvenile literature.
Classification: LCC BF723.A25 I8413 2020 | DDC 155.4/139--dc23
LC record available at https://lccn.loc.gov/2019048110

VN0004589; 9781506463193; JAN2020

Beaming Books
510 Marquette Avenue
Minneapolis, MN 55402
Beamingbooks.com

THE BIG BOOK OF
SUPER
POWERS

WRITTEN BY **SUSANNA ISERN**   ILLUSTRATED BY **ROCIO BONILLA**

beaming books
MINNEAPOLIS

Rocio Bonilla holds a BFA and worked in advertising for many years before founding her own company, Once Upon a Time, which creates murals for children's rooms.

Susanna Isern has published over sixty books worldwide, translated into over a dozen languages. She has been awarded the Silver Medal in the Moonbeam Children's Book Awards. She works as a child psychologist and writer.

THE BIG BOOK OF
SUPER POWERS

WRITTEN BY **SUSANNA ISERN**   ILLUSTRATED BY **ROCIO BONILLA**

beaming ☼ books

MINNEAPOLIS

"And at that exact moment, a dark shadow appeared behind her. It was as big as a tree, but also as slippery as a snake. She turned slowly and . . ."

Everyone shivers. Their eyes open wide. Their hair stands on end, and their hearts pound. When Elena tells a horror story, everyone trembles in terror.

When Elena tells a funny story, their laughs burst out of control. If she describes an incredible adventure, everyone lives it as if they were the hero of the story. And if it's about love, her listeners cry until they soak their handkerchiefs.

With her stories, Elena transports her audience to other worlds. They forget their worries for a little while.

Elena's superpower is
STORYTELLING.

His mouth is always shaped like an orange slice. He walks with a spring in his step, humming a happy song to himself. Marc brings joy wherever he goes. When he's around, the daisies bloom, the birds sing, and even timid creatures come out of their dens to watch him pass by.

Marc seems to wear magic glasses to help him see the glass as half full. If he runs out of water in the middle of crossing a desert, he keeps going until the next dune. Sooner or later he'll encounter an oasis! And if dark storm clouds approach, Marc grabs an umbrella and gets on his bicycle. He pedals and pedals until he finds the sunlight.

Marc's superpower is OPTIMISM.

Nora is afraid of a lot of things. Sometimes that's good because it keeps her safe. But sometimes being afraid stops her from doing what she needs and wants to do. In times like these, Nora takes a deep breath, fills herself with strength, and bravely decides to face her fears.

If she has to get a shot at the doctor's office or stand up in front of the whole class at school, Nora plucks up her courage and does it boldly. If she wants to get on the fast roller coaster or enter the hair-raising House of Horrors, Nora thinks about the adventure and gets on the rides without a second thought. No matter the challenge, Nora faces it and reaches for the stars.

Nora's superpower is COURAGE.

"What's that?" "A flock of swallows?"

"No, it's Marina's music."

When Marina plays the violin, the notes waft out the window. They flutter around like birds, bringing a smile to the face of everyone who passes by. Everyone who hears Marina's beautiful melodies feels a little happier.

Marina's music is so beautiful that even animals turn quiet and listen when they hear it. Her melodies bring back memories and pluck emotions from the hearts of her listeners.

Marina's superpower is MUSIC.

She always greets bad weather with her best smile. If she slips on a banana peel, she roars with laughter. If a bird leaves a little "gift" in her hair, she thinks that's a sign of good luck. If she falls into a puddle she realizes it's a great opportunity to splash and play in the water.

Lucía laughs and makes others laugh. Everyone loves having her around. She carries a bunch of funny jokes in her backpack. She hides a handful of clever (but always harmless!) pranks under her hat. But most of all, she has brilliant ideas to deal with small problems with laughter and good cheer.

Lucía's superpower is HUMOR.

They say his eyes are like magnifying glasses. His ears are like satellite dishes. His nose is like high-precision radar. And his skin is a powerful detector of shapes, sizes, textures, and temperatures.

Carlos can see one red fire ant among a million black ants. He can hear the jingle of a lost cat's bell amid the noise of the loud birthday party. Carlos never misses a thing!

Carlos's superpower is ATTENTION.

Yuna has a super-special jacket with hidden pockets and invisible zippers to carry her gadgets: binoculars to see the bottom of a river, a magnifying glass to look at tiny things, a compass that helps her go exploring, a mud-proof notebook, some clothespins . . .

What Yuna likes best is to go for a walk in the woods or explore a museum and make new and incredible discoveries. How many feet does a centipede actually have? Is there life on other planets? Do giant octopuses exist?

Yuna's superpower is CURIOSITY.

Time seems to pass differently for Daniel. Maybe that's why he can wait so long for what he wants: finding a four-leaf clover in a big meadow, seeing a mouse stick its head up from a hole in the ground, or waiting for a cup of hot chocolate to cool to the right temperature so he doesn't burn his tongue.

Daniel is also an expert in keeping his cool. That's why he doesn't let himself get carried away when he gets annoyed with someone. He can deal with the most complicated situations calmly and resolve them the right way.

Daniel's superpower is PATIENCE.

There are piles of books in Mateo's house. On his bed, in the closets, on the sofas, even in the washing machine! There's not one spot on the walls that doesn't have a bookshelf. And if that weren't enough, the clothes Mateo wears have huge pockets where he stashes his latest reads.

Mateo reads all the time and knows lots of things. He never feels alone and never gets bored. It doesn't matter how; it doesn't matter where—he reads and travels to magic worlds. He sails the seas aboard a pirate ship. His hair stands on end as he walks through a haunted house. He solves the hardest mysteries like a true detective.

Mateo's superpower is READING.

She rescues kittens trapped in tree branches by jumping as high as a kangaroo. Even if she's late, she never misses the bus, because she can run as fast as a cheetah. When she takes a dip in the ocean, she swims like a dolphin, leaping from wave to wave, discovering treasures hidden in the depths.

It doesn't matter if she's moving on land, sea, or air: when it comes to agility, Claudia can do anything she wants. One summer she climbed hundreds of steps up a very high tower without getting tired—just to watch a splendid show of shooting stars. And once she ran many miles to alert neighbors to a dangerous fire. She was running so fast you could hardly see her legs!

Claudia's superpower is AGILITY.

Alberto has a memory as big as an elephant's. He remembers everything he reads from start to finish. If someone doesn't have a place to write down a phone number or even a long message, Alberto is there with his giant memory. He makes a note of it quickly in his head.

Alberto's mind is like a camera. That's why he can remember even the smallest details: the colors of all the socks of all the students in his class, the number of freckles a classmate has, the names of all the dogs on his block. With his memory, Alberto can learn countless things to use when he needs them most.

Alberto's superpower is MEMORY.

Sofía is so organized, in the blink of an eye she could find a tiny bead in a drawer where she keeps a thousand trinkets. Or find a book with a spine as thin as a thread in the middle of a huge, overstuffed bookcase.

But best of all, Sofía can plan her weekly schedule so well that she always has time left over to read, play, rest, or visit her friends. Sofía also organizes parties that everyone wants to attend, with clowns, exciting athletic contests and races, thrilling stories, and treats brought from all over the world.

Sofía's superpower is ORGANIZATION.

Sergio has a collection of little jars where he stores secret, special ingredients that he picks up along his way. A piece of this, a little pinch of that . . . He uses these ingredients to cook the most incredible recipes you can imagine.

Once he baked a cake that was so big and spongy, you could have slept on it. Another time he made a soup using ingredients that were all the colors of the rainbow. No matter what food is in the refrigerator, Sergio knows how to put it together and cook it into a dish that dazzles the eye and tastes delicious! Feeding his friends is his favorite thing in the whole world.

Sergio's superpower is COOKING.

Laura is like a chameleon. She can thrive almost anywhere and adapt to deal with almost anything. If she has to visit the North Pole, Laura puts on a warm coat to survive icy winds. If the challenge is to cross a desert, Laura wears a hat to block out the sun and rides her camel across the dunes.

It doesn't matter if she has to live in a village nestled in the mountains or among big-city skyscrapers. It's all the same to her if she sleeps on a mattress in a fancy hotel or on the hard ground when she goes camping. At school, she adjusts to every new assignment and challenge that comes her way. Laura always adjusts with a smile to new circumstances—even if they seem difficult at first.

Laura's superpower is ADAPTABILITY.

It doesn't matter if on his path he finds a high stone wall or a puddle so big the water soaks his shoes. Or if he starts feeling tired after having traveled many miles.

Leo's not one to leave things half-done. If he gets tired, he stops to regain his strength. And if he hears the voice of discouragement, he puts some good earplugs in his ears and ignores it. Leo never gives up. He follows his path, come rain or shine, until he reaches his goal.

Leo's superpower is PERSEVERANCE.

"If 30 waves hit the beach in one minute, how many waves will hit it in one hour?"

"1,800 waves!" replies Carlota, in a flash.

"If you've caught 365 crabs, but you still need 498, how many crabs do you need total?"

"863 crabs!" Carlota responds, fast as lightning.

It doesn't matter how many digits a number has. Or if she's dealing with addition, multiplication, or a division problem. Numbers jump and dance at top speed in her head, as if she is a human calculator. It takes Carlota less than one second to give the right answer. But best of all is her ability to determine the possibility of something happening. How likely is it that it will rain this weekend? What are the chances that she will win the prize in a drawing?

Carlota's superpower is MATH.

A tap-dancing outfit, ballet shoes, a pair of tights, a pair of sneakers. Or anything from the closet and bare feet. If he needs a partner, he uses a pillow, a broom, or the cat!

And when Pablo dances, everything starts moving as if by magic. Cups and plates rattle, clothes fly, animals wag their tails and whiskers to the beat. Even the ground trembles, causing a small earthquake. Pablo dances down the sidewalk, in the rain, or on the ice (very carefully!). And while he's dancing, he is truly happy: nothing can erase the smile from his face.

Pablo's superpower is DANCE.

He builds a birdhouse with a cardboard box. He uses an upside-down umbrella as a boat for squirrels to cross the river. He uses dried leaves to draw the forest, animals, trees, and even caves where sleeping bears hide. He collects and paints different objects, making them into a useful pencil case, an eight-armed octopus coat rack, or a magician's hat.

Where others see a blank sheet of paper, Adri sees an airplane in flight, a boat ride, or a train trip. A paintbrush and a box of watercolors are the gateway to a new world for him. And when he learns a new word, he uses it to create an exciting and amazing story. Adri even finds original solutions to the most complicated problems.

Adri's superpower is CREATIVITY.

These are the **SUPERPOWERS** that appear in the book.

WHICH ARE YOURS?

- STORYTELLING
- OPTIMISM
- COURAGE
- MUSIC
- HUMOR
- ATTENTION
- CURIOSITY
- PATIENCE
- READING
- AGILITY
- MEMORY
- ORGANIZATION
- COOKING
- ADAPTABILITY
- PERSEVERANCE
- MATH
- DANCE
- CREATIVITY

We don't have to have just one superpower. We can have many!

Think about your own **SUPERPOWERS**.

Then get out a piece of paper and write out a story

for yourself like the ones in this book. What are your superpowers?

You probably have some that aren't even on the list!